LOVE UNFATHOMABLE

KRISHNA BAGARIA

ISBN 978-93-5458-191-5
© KRISHNA BAGARIA 2021
Published in India 2021 by Pencil

A brand of
One Point Six Technologies Pvt. Ltd.
123, Building J2, Shram Seva Premises,
Wadala Truck Terminal, Wadala (E)
Mumbai 400037, Maharashtra, INDIA
E connect@thepencilapp.com
W www.thepencilapp.com

Author biography

I'm Krishna Bagaria, and before moving to Kolkata, I was born and raised in Nepal. I am currently a 2nd year B.com (Hons) student.

I've enrolled in a variety of courses, including dance, cricket, and chess, all of which have helped me improve my health and knowledge.

My main goal is to travel the world and write about it, as well as to convey the beauty of India through my writing so that everyone can learn about it.

I enjoy a variety of activities, including listening to music, swimming.

CONTENTS

Acknowledgements

First and foremost, I want to express my gratitude to my family for not giving up on me and for encouraging me to write a novel. I'd also like to thank several people who have assisted me in entering this profession and who have encouraged me to write this book.

In addition, I'd like to express my gratitude to Raunak Saraff, who served as both my editor and advisor in this area, As well as Bhumika Saraff for helping me out in editing the story.

I couldn't have done it without your help and enthusiasm.

A special thanks to the school teachers who have helped me in this endeavour. I'd like to express my gratitude to Pencil for assisting me in this area and assisting me with the publication of my book.

I would like to express my gratitude to my teachers, Ankit Kumar Jaiswal and AngshumanSarma, for their assistance in this area.

I'd like to thank all of the readers for taking the time to read it.

Introduction

It's a love story between two people and how their friends and family help them. They are together in life after all the difficulties faced by them. Before diving into the story,
Let me tell you the main points of the story.
Firstly, to know the importance of work, as being financially independent is a very essential in life,
Secondly, the distance and the space never reduce love from our hearts. It demonstrates that, in the end, love triumphs over differences and distances.
It's a joy when school love which is also a first love ends up with flying colour. In this tale, the challenge and situation they encountered is elaborated, as well as why the circumstances occurred they went apart should be understood.
The story's goals and morals can also be deduced from this story.
This story is more than a story; it is a life lesson.
Now let's continue with the novel, and I hope you enjoy it.

MY INSPIRATION AND HOW DID I GET THE IDEA TO WRITE A BOOK

My inspiration for writing came from my friend Raunak Saraff.

He suggested that I should write down my thoughts in a copy. As I continued to write, I gained a wealth of knowledge and experience. Then I began blogging and writing on my Instagram account, where I could gain experience and get feedback from my peers.

I've entered many poetry and creative writing contests to develop my skills. To develop my skills in this area, I also enrolled in a creative writing course at My Captain's.

I was researching and gaining experience in this area at the same time. My sisters suggested that I start reading books to widen my scope. I decided to read a book called "Can Love Happen Twice?" After reading the novel, my quest for a love story sparked a lot of creativity. So I decided to write them all down. When I was researching, I had no idea that I was going to publish a novel. After a lot of hardwork, the book was completed.

Finally, I believe that we should aspire to improve in all aspects of our lives because we are never the best. The truth is that we are competent in a field, and continuous progress is the only way to achieve success.

1st Chapter

It's July 6, 2013, and all of their high school friends are getting together after a long time to attend a school friend's wedding. Outside the entrance, a sign read, "Rajdeep weds Krinjal."

They stared at the sign and started recalling the past. Sam, Rahul, Saiyam, Minakshi, and Ariyan were five friends who attended Delhi Public School.

They talked about their time in class, how they bunked classes, fought with each other, made fun of teachers and enjoyed their school life.

Before going forward, let me tell you how they were during their school days.

2nd Chapter

They were all so different. Sam was a laid-back guy who loved spending time with his family and friends and avoided getting himself into any trouble. He was a devout student at the university.

Rahul, on the other hand, was completely different.

He was just a quiet person who never spoke to anyone and was always absent from class. He was terrified of everybody.

Saiyam was a chatty young man who was the school's most intolerant person. He was known for making fun of both teachers and students. He didn't give a damn about what other people thought. He was well-known. Minakshi was a lovely young lady who exuded innocence. She was, however, a flirty person.

Ariyan, last but not least, was a traveller. He had travelled to many places since he was a child and was an excellent photographer.

They were all roommates at the hostel where they met. Rajesh and Krinjal were two more people with them. We'll discuss them in the second half of the story.

3rd Chapter

They had strange judgements about each other the first time they met because each person was so different from the other. After a few days, Rajesh and Sam had formed a strong bond. Krinjal and Minakshi used to talk about the boys, whine about them, and pass judgements on them. Ariyan and Saiyam will constantly fought.

Sam and, Rajesh, as well as Minakshi and Krinjal, quickly became best friends.

So, let's get this story started. So, how is it?

How are Rajdeep and Krinjal getting along these days?

The relationship began with a school-sponsored picnic.

That's how it all began. Let's see where this goes and how it all ends.

4th Chapter

It was an once-in-a-lifetime experience for those who were present at the picnic spot. The students had been invited to a lavish picnic by their school. When they arrived, they went to their tent and stored their belongings. They were hungry after all of their travelling's, so they ate at a restaurant and then went for a walk in the forest. They went to bed after that because it was late and they had plans to go for a hike and watch the sunrise from the top of the hill the next morning.

5th Chapter

The night, on the other hand, was unforgettable for everyone. After everyone had gone to bed, two or three students sneaked out to have some fun. The students in the tents were all startled when they suddenly heard a loud, potentially dangerous noise. This woke them up. They went outside to investigate the noise.

Then there was a forest inspector who assured them that it was just an animal's echo. An instructor found that three students were absent as they were conversing.

6th Chapter

During the hunt for the students, their belongings were discovered in the forest. They found a watch on the board, as well as some clothing. Since there were wild animals in the area, everybody was terrified of what could have happened to them. When the teacher returned after a long search, they were terrified because the student's duty was now theirs.

However, when the students return from the forest after a while, their clothes were completely ripped. Rajdeep was the most seriously injured among the three.

7th Chapter

Krinjal had been greatly affected by this incident because she loved him for quite a long time but had never told anyone except Minakshi about it. However, everyone knew she liked Rajdeep after seeing her get stressed about him that day. That day, both of them decided to start dating, as Rajdeep confessed while he saw love in Minakshi's eyes, as Rajdeep too liked her but kept it as a secret.

When the teacher confronted and scolded them for going to the forest without permission, they explained that an animal pursued them and how they were wounded while running and trying to get away from the animal. Since the incident was so dangerous, the instructor feared for the other students' safety, so they came back the next morning.

8th Chapter

Their school and hostel experiences were fantastic. Their friends mocked Rajdeep and Minakshi all the time. All pitched in to help them skip classes so they could spend more time together. They were so in love that they would always take each other's side, no matter who was against them. The school teacher became enraged and reprimanded them by separating them into separate classes.

Their quarters had been rearranged as well. But they were so close that they managed to get away from the teachers and meet each other under unusual circumstances.

9th Chapter

Their relationship had been strained because they couldn't see each other. An instructor discovered them skipping classes and fooling around one day. Their academic performance was also deplorable. Teachers were forced to tell their parents due to deplorable performance, their parents made the decision to move them to a different school. As a result, they were both unhappy and had been apart for a long time.

Sam went to see Rajdeep one day, and when he arrived, Rajdeep was sad and unstable. His parents had been looking for Krinjal to assist him, but she had moved her school and he had lost touch with her.

10th Chapter

Sam went looking for Krinjal and obtained her phone number from Minakshi. He came to know that she had left the country and moved to the United States. They had no idea where she was in the United States, so they used social media to track her down. They noticed a girl named Rupsa who looked like her and later discovered she was Krijal. Krinjal was stressed about the smallest of items, but no one wanted to tell her about Rajdeep's condition because she had just begun her new journey and was very content. But then she inquired about Rajdeep, and they were forced to inform her. Kinjal began to be concerned about her high school crush and began making plans.

11th Chapter

She asked her parents if she can go to Lucknow because Rajdeep was staying there and told them about his situation, but they refused because she was doing such a good job in the US. Her parents didn't want her to waste time on trivial matters.

A week later, Rajdeep approached Sam and inquired about Krinjal. Sam told him everything he needed to know about Krinjal. He was so enamoured with her that he thought of going in search for her in the United States. He attempted to reach her via her social media account, but it was no longer active.

12th Chapter

Rajdeep managed to figure out the location of Krinjal and he went and stayed at a hotel nearby. When Krinjal found out about him, she secretly rushed to the hotel to meet him. By looking at his condition, she couldn't believe that Rajdeep was not able to talk to anyone and was enormously hurt by it. Rajdeep was not in good condition and needed care. Krinjal had an important and urgent meeting to attend, so she trusted and called her parents to look after Rajdeep before she returned.

13th Chapter

Krinjal's kin, on the other hand, had other ideas. After speaking with her parents, he left the area and went somewhere without telling anyone. He wrote Krinjal a letter that read, "Hey Krinjal, I am glad to see that you are doing well. However, I have some important work. I just came to see you once. I don't want you to worry about me. I shall meet you soon. Yours truly, Rajdeep. "

14th Chapter

As a result, no one knew where he was after that day. What he was doing, where he was. Only thing he did was inform his family and friends that he would come after one to two years. His family and friends attempted to reach him but received no response. Sam was the only one who knew about him, and he was told not to tell anyone.

Days passed and everything was back to normal. The group of DPS decided to have a reunion of the school roommates. They tried to inform Rajdeep too, through his phone number, but no response was there from him. On the day of the reunion, while everyone was present, Krinjal didn't seem to come. But after a while, there was a knock at the door.

15th Chapter

Krinjal was there as soon as the door opened, and everyone greeted her warmly. She was more beautiful than ever before, and she was a successful businesswoman. They were both taken aback when they saw her. Everyone was commenting on how she had changed and considered starting her own company.

She told them about what happened after that incident and how her life changed as a result of it. Her parents inquired as to whether she wanted to attend a boarding school or continue her education in the United States. So she chose the second choice and embarked on a journey to better herself, but she was warned not to contact Rajdeep. She completed her college education there.She was offered a job interview by her college after graduation, which she accepted and passed. Her life was beginning to change. Then she recalls the incident, when Rajdeep came to meet her, she received an opportunity to advance her career from a large corporation. She recalled leaving Rajdeep with her parents to attend that particular meeting. She also told them about the incident at the hotel, where her parents had urged Rajdeep to be ambitious so that he could make a name for himself in Krinjal life.

16th Chapter

School memories were exchanged. They discussed life after, where they are now, and what has been going on in their lives.

Rajdeep called Sam months later to inquire about his family and friends. He inquired about Krinjal and the specifics of the school reunion. They discussed the events of the day and how he took a stand on the road to success after his conversation with Krinjals' parents. Sam inquired about his intentions to return home, but he remained silent and only asked him to look after his family. He intended to return after he had completed all of his tasks.

After a few month,Rajdeep told Sam to inform his family and friends, as well as Krinjal, about his well-being. Rajdeep's parents were relieved to know that he was doing well and were grateful to see his friends rallying behind him. They had been closely knit since childhood and knew how emotional Rajdeep was. They were, however, worried about him and did not want him to take the wrong step if he didn't find success.

17th Chapter

They decided to track him down and contacted Saiyam, who was now a well-known police officer. He traced the phone number from which Rajdeep called Sam, and they discovered he was in Delhi. They travelled to Delhi in order to know more about Rajdeep and return him to his family. They went to the location where he called Sam and began looking for him by flashing his photo around the neighbourhood. They discovered that he was staying in a cottage after a lengthy search.

18th Chapter

They discovered the cottage's location but it was closed. When his neighbours inquired about him, they learned that he was working for a marketing consulting firm and had been promoted to a high position. Following up on their inquiries about him, they came to know that he had been in the hospital for 3 to 4 days due to high blood pressure. They hurried to the hospital in the hopes of finding him. Rajdeep was surprised to see them, but he was also relieved to be able to communicate with them, and he requested that they not inform his family about his condition.

19th Chapter

He was scheduled to be released from the hospital at 6 p.m., but they stayed at the hospital to await the doctor's confirmation. His friends bombarded him with questions after he was released from the hospital. Rajdeep was surprised to see them, but he was also relieved to be able to communicate with them, and he requested that they not inform his family about his condition. He was scheduled to be released from the hospital at 6 p.m., but they stayed at the hospital to await the doctor's confirmation. His friends bombarded him with questions after he was released from the hospital.

20th Chapter

Her parents' fears were justified. He recognised his error and resolved to live a safe and fruitful life so that he could be proud of himself in front of his parents. He returned to Delhi in search of work. He had 20,000 rupees and had purchased a cottage for himself. He had a strong command of the English language and a broad vocabulary, which contributed to a position with an article writing firm. He received a call from a marketing consulting firm offering him a position two or three months later. He had been employed for almost a year and was in a decent position, earning well. He had intended to visit Krinjals' parents the next week, but he became ill and was admitted to the hospital.

21st Chapter

Rajdeep and his friends from a childhood spent a week in Delhi. It was exactly as it had been in the past. After a week, he returned to the United States, as expected, in search of her and to speak with her parents. Krinjal, on the other hand, was nowhere to be found. He had previously been unable to locate her at her previous residence. He went from place to place looking for her, asking people in the area but had no idea about it. He attempted to contact her using the number he received from a friend, but it was unreachable. He returned home after giving up hope of ever finding her, but he continued to search for her every day. His life had been a struggle. He had tried everything he could to make her dream come true, but nothing he tried yielded a satisfactory result. His family was ecstatic that he had achieved success and was doing well in life. He was also planning to relocate from Delhi to Lucknow.

22nd Chapter

Krinjal had called to wish Rajdeep a happy 26th birthday. He was overjoyed to be speaking with her. They had a great 2 to 3-hour chat with each other. Sam had informed her of all the things he had done for her through social media, and she felt fortunate to have someone in her life who understood her. She invited him to visit her in the United States. He grabbed his tickets and left right away. They had a great week together, spending time with each other and passing the time like they used to. Both were overjoyed to find such a supportive partner.

He was always supposed to speak with her parents, though. He was very apprehensive about the discussion he was about to have.

23rd Chapter

He was going to meet her parents again. He was aware of the potential outcomes of the discussion, but to his surprise, his parents were warm and accepting. They were pleased to see him succeed, and they were pleased that their daughter would be with someone who had worked from dawn to dusk and lived alone in Delhi, ensuring that she would not face any difficulties in her life. They knew he'd be there for her and would be her rock. They set a date for their wedding. They were grateful for their friends' help, which allowed them to spend time together.

The Conclusion

Rajdeep and Krinjal had their ups and downs as well. They were engaged on November 25, 2012, and married on July 6, 2013. It took both of them a long time and a lot of commitment to be together in their lives, but it all worked out well in the end.

The moral of the story

The story's moral is that
You should have a friend like Sam, who is there in your tough times.
The significance of work in one's life is important, to provide a decent life for one's family as well as to make an image of themselves.
Last but not least, distance does not change the beauty of love, and their love was unaffected by their patience or the gap between them.